TALONS

TALONS

By
TL KATT

A story from the Winter
Thrillz Collection.

TALONS

Published by Books by Elle, Inc.
225 College Dr. #65504
Orange Park, FL 32065
www.elleklass.weebly.com

Chapter 1

r. Meg Mercer walked out of the hospital's double glass doors into the brisk evening. The only thought on her mind getting home to spend an hour with Amy before bed. Within a few paces of her Mercedes, a large shadow darkened the air surrounding her, slicing the atmosphere above her. She lifted her head upwards and a chill

TALONS

crawled down her spine. Before she could react, talon-like fingers wrapped firmly onto her shoulders. The blade of each talon gripped her securely under the arms. She screamed and wriggled against their grip, causing a stinging sensation as the talons cut into her armpits.

Her screams of protest went unheard as the parking lot was barren of onlookers. The beast with the talons lifted her off the ground and was soon high in the air, the objects below her growing smaller as her feet brushed the tips of a small cluster of trees. She struggled against it, her feet flailing in the air. The more she struggled, the deeper the talons sank. Shooting pains ripped through her body. The strength of the beast's grasp far outweighed her meager efforts to dislodge herself.

Amy! Meg screamed as her body drifted higher into the air. Tears escaped her eyes, freezing to her face upon contact with the frigid air. The beast carried her higher into the clouds. Its wings creating a steady swooshing

TALONS

sound. The houses and buildings of the city appearing as tiny Lego homes beneath her.

The more she struggled, the more futile the battle was as the creature's talons only served to grip her tighter. Twisting her head, she could see nothing above her but clouds, and trees and mountains below. The high altitude air wrapped around her body like a frozen blanket. Shivers danced across her skin and drove their icicle claws deep into her bones. One of the creature's talons drove forcefully into her right armpit causing a sharp pain that echoed through her body. A guttural scream escaped her mouth and she lay limp, hanging from the beast's arms.

TALONS
Chapter 2

Meg stirred in her bed. Her eyelids fluttered from the noonday brightness of the sun flooding through her windows. Radiation traveled across her skin forcing the illusion that she was on fire. Leaping out of bed in one smooth movement she swept the curtains together, blocking out the light. She could remember the beast snagging her off the ground and his sharp talons which dug sharply into her, but not how she made it to her bed. Perched on the edge of her bed, she cupped her face in her hands and convinced herself it was all a dream.

"Miss Meg, I hear you stirring and brought some coffee. Two spoons of sugar and a dab of creamer just the way you like," said Elsa, Amy's nanny, as she opened the door a sliver.

"Thank-you, Elsa."

"You decent?"

"Come in, honey." Elsa had been with the family from the time Amy was born. She was far more than a nanny, supporting Meg as she grieved the loss of her husband and loving Amy as her own when Meg had been too devastated to make it out of bed.

"Oh, Miss Meg, you don't look good. Your cheeks are flushed red like a tomato." Elsa placed the coffee on the nightstand beside the bed and brought her hand to Meg's forehead. Worry wrinkles creased her chocolate hairline and brow. "You're burning up, and what are all those splotches on your legs and arms? We need to cool you down!" Elsa ran out of the room, leaving Meg to stare at her body covered in splashes of red inflamed skin. A fever and illness would explain the hallucinations she dreamt the night before.

Within minutes, Elsa returned with a cold cloth that she placed on Meg's forehead. "This will cool you off while I draw your bath." Like a small black whirlwind, Elsa had the bath water running and was slipping off Meg's gown and lowering her into the tub of chilly oatmeal water. Meg knew

TALONS

better than to resist Elsa's efforts and complied.

Shivering beneath the cold water brought her back to her dream and the frozen air. She could almost feel the large talons beneath her armpits and the acute pain the creature's claw had caused. She brought her left hand instinctively to beneath her under arm and felt a hole the size of her pinky. She removed her hand and drew her arm up over her head. "Elsa, do you see anything?"

Elsa's eyes grew twice their average size.

"What happened?" she asked, bringing her fat fingers to the hole and rubbing gently across it. "Does it hurt?"

"No, it's just a big hole. It feels like someone stuck me with a centimeter-sized needle."

Elsa reached over and grabbed a vanity mirror off the counter and positioned it where Meg could see the hole. She stared at it, her mouth gaping with fear as she realized last night had not been a dream. She had been abducted by something that stuck her and most likely drugged

TALONS

her. She couldn't go to the hospital with this, not after the disappearance of her husband and the mystery that surrounded the strange death of the man thought to have been guilty of murdering several people. No, she was a doctor and would take and analyze her own tox screen.

"Elsa, help me out of the tub, I have work to do!" Sensing the urgency of her tone, Elsa did as asked, against her own judgement. Meg was her friend but also her employer. Meg threw her bathrobe on and rushed through the house with lightning speed, not stopping as she yelled, "Tell Amy I had to leave town for a few days." Her voice trailed off, leaving Elsa seated on the lip of the tub in a quandary.

As Meg sped through the house, she could feel the sun's heat nipping at her skin even though a thin layer of snow covered the ground. She had no time to close the drapes to the many floor to ceiling windows that enclosed her home. She had fallen in love with the large amounts of sunlight that streamed in, giving

TALONS

the house a warm, cozy
feel -- but not now.
Today, she hated the light
and the tendrils of heat
that ebbed across her
exposed skin. With a
speed far beyond her
ability, she was but a mere
flash streaking through
the home.

In the basement, she
tore through boxes of lab
equipment; setting aside
test tubes, needles, flasks,
a hot plate, and
microscope. She had used
the equipment to analyze
the sample her colleague
and college dorm mate --
now FBI lab rat -- had
collected from the

sociopath's blood. The sample had been small but enough to tell her the toxin he was injected with was unknown and deadly to him. When it interacted with his blood, within seconds the agent destroyed every blood cell in his body. It acted as a virus exploding each red blood cell from the inside out like over inflated balloons. Yet when she mixed the toxin with her own blood it mingled, restructuring the hemoglobin protein in a way that allowed it to carry more oxygen throughout the body.

TALONS

Meg found the large bulging vein in her arm. Without hesitation, she withdrew a vial of blood.

Chapter 3

Several hours after locking herself in the basement and running every test she had the materials and ability to complete, she hadn't been able to identify the toxin in her blood. Her skin, on the other hand, had cleared up. Every splotch had disappeared and her skin became a couple shades lighter than its usual paleness.

Meg stared at the small sample of the toxin

that had killed the sociopath. Only a couple drops remained, but all she needed was one. With a syringe, she gathered a miniscule amount of the unknown toxin and lifted it above a slide containing a sample of her own blood. She was hoping for the same response she got four years ago. She squeezed the drop onto the slide, then adjusted the microscope. It took a matter of a few seconds for her blood cells to explode. Her body shuddered involuntarily as she realized whatever the sociopath had been she was now the same.

Meg feared the worst, that she would become like him, savagely draining the blood of others. Her home and Amy weren't safe with her here. A collection of suitcases and a small overnight bag sat near the base of the steps. Unzipping the overnight bag, she collected a sample of her own blood and slid it into a pouch inside. When Amy was in bed, she would make her way upstairs, collect a few items, place a bundle of cash and a credit card in

TALONS

the drawer for Elsa to care for Amy until her return. She cringed at the thought of never returning and vowed to herself, *Amy, I will be back for you, I promise.*

At nine p.m. when she knew Amy was safely tucked into bed, she wrapped a towel across her face in case her disease was airborne, crept up the stairs and gently pushed the door open. The scent of meatloaf and turnip greens blasted her nostrils and reminded her that she had not eaten all day. She didn't have time now, but would be sure to have Elsa pack a small container.

Meg threw a pair of sweatpants, jeans and a couple T-shirts into her bag along with a few toiletries and a brush. Still wearing her bathrobe, she pulled it off and slipped on a comfortable pair of jeans and a baggy shirt. On tiptoe, she went to Amy's room and popped her head in. Amy was sound asleep. The cover bundled up to her chin; her curls spread out across her pillow. She looked like a tiny angel. Meg was near positive

TALONS

that her disease was passed through blood but wasn't willing to take any chances and give Amy a kiss. Her entire being begged her to hug the child tightly and never let go, but she shoved the urge aside, not willing to possibly infect her darling daughter and continued down the hallway to Elsa's room.

As she approached the door, she heard the TV in the background. Carefully she pushed the door aside. "Elsa, we need to talk."

Immediately Elsa came to the door and,

upon observing her appearance, asked, "Meg, the splotches are gone, but your skin -- it's so pale, albino pale. Your eyes too, they aren't sapphire blue, but more of a pale gray-blue. Please tell me what I can do." Worry laced the tone of her voice.

"I have to leave and I need you to care for Amy. I will place money and a credit card into the top desk drawer in the den. I don't know how long I will be." Concern and fear filled every word that spilled from her mouth.

TALONS

"You shouldn't be going anywhere but the hospital. Look at you, your skin, your eyes. Turn around please."

Meg followed her directive and turned around then spun back quickly. Elsa took her hands and patted Meg's sides. "You have shrunk. Look how baggy your clothes are." Meg followed her to the mirror and lifted her shirt, revealing a body that Meg hadn't seen in five years. "You need medical care. Please, as your friend, let me drive you. We don't have to tell Amy. She is too young to understand, but you need help and medicine. Whatever this is, I fear it's worse than cancer." Elsa had seen Meg distraught with the loss of her husband but even then she hadn't looked so sickly.

Meg understood the anxiety in Elsa's voice. She felt it too. After what she had seen with her own eyes, she couldn't take herself to the hospital. She may have some type of chemical or biological agent inside her and be the study for tests that would prove nothing, while making the entire staff and all the patients deathly ill. "I can't. I have to solve this one on my own." Her eyes pleaded for understanding.

"Meg, I love Amy and am more than happy to care for her. Tell me you are coming back?"

"I will. It's my promise to you and Amy." Tears filled her eyes and trickled down her cheek.

Matching tears streamed down Elsa's face as she reached over to hug Meg, who jumped backwards as if tazered by a jolt of electricity. Meg placed her hand out in front of her. "No." She shook her head, no, as if to emphasize the point. The hurt look in Elsa's eyes made her heart cry. "I'm sick, very sick and I could be contagious." That was the reason she gave Elsa -- mostly the truth. She also had a deep desire to sink her teeth into Elsa's pulsing artery. The scent of her blood had wafted through Meg's nostrils and a primordial desire almost took control. She quickly exited the room before she did something she would most definitely regret.

TALONS

While Meg stuffed a wad of cash and a credit card along with the keys to the Mercedes in the desk drawer, Elsa packed her several days' worth of food, mostly meats and vegetables. She felt Meg needed the iron, vitamins, and minerals to keep her strength in order to fight her illness.

Meg kept her distance, grabbed her few items which she threw into the back seat of her dead husband's Jeep. She knew an all-terrain vehicle would be better for her trip and maneuvering through the snow than the Mercedes. She had decided upon calling her FBI lab rat friend to hand over the vial of her blood. Of course, she would lie and say it belonged to a patient.

TALONS
Chapter 4

eatloaf aroma tantalized Meg's senses and awoke a craving inside her that had been dormant for four years. Her female organs felt alive and dripped with passion. With a quick jerk, she pulled over the Jeep, dust and rocks flew in all directions. She ripped the top off the container and plunged her head inside gorging on the meat which felt tender against her tongue and made her taste buds water. The delectable morsel of meatloaf was only enough to send her body into a meat frenzy. She tore into all the containers, devouring each bit of meat; licking the sides of each dish until no more meat remained. When she had polished it off, her body convulsed in waves of ecstasy, a shrill scream filled with desire forced its way through her vocal chords and echoed through the trees.

When the surge of pent up euphoria left her; she lay slumped across the front seats-- spent. A growing feeling crept inside her and she raised her head, feeling dirty. Containers, lids, and vegetables were strewn across the seats and carpets of the Jeep. A small bit of a broccoli head fell onto her nose and landed in her crotch. She quickly swiped it away and looked upwards to glance at the headliner. It was caked in broccoli, mashed potatoes, and turnip greens.

Meg grabbed a T-shirt out of her bag and wiped as much of the food away as she could.

Her husband had always kept the Jeep impeccably clean and, in only a few minutes, she had destroyed everything he worked for, decimating his memory. Her eyes welled up with liquid sorrow and short breaths followed by sighs filled her lungs.

After a few minutes of collecting her emotions, she called her lab rat FBI friend Gery. The number rang several times and just as she was about to hang up, she heard, "Hello, Meg?"

"Gery, how are you?" She didn't want to

rush into, *Can I bring you a sample.*

"It's late. You didn't call for small talk. What's the problem?" Gery had never been much for small talk and had the social graces of a computer.

"Um… I came across something odd at the hospital. I was hoping you could analyze it for me?" Meg checked the time and cringed for calling so late. She should have waited until the morning.

"You know I can do that for you. What time would you like to meet?"

"First, you need to know something about the blood. It may be carrying a virus -- some type of biological agent." Upon saying the words, Meg suddenly felt a twinge of guilt. "You know, it's okay." Gery cut her off.

"Meg, that's my specialty. I know you, and you're bearing the weight of a million souls on your shoulders. I can handle this. My lab is set up for it. Where are you?" Gery knew for her friend to call this late it was important and she could hear the urgency in her voice.

TALONS

"West Virginia. I can be in Arlington in an hour. Meet me at Crazy Eights Coffee?" Gery could hear the tension and hesitation in her friend's voice. She knew trouble was near. Out of concern, she agreed to meet her. What she didn't tell her was that she was bringing along muscle; her personal trainer and brother, Kent.

Chapter 5

As soon as Gery hung up, she threw the closest pair of jeans and a sweatshirt over her braless chest. She called Kent on her way to his house. He was waiting outside, his biceps and chest muscles bulging through every available opening of his tank. He had been a scrawny kid until a few years ago. She couldn't place the exact date. It was a near overnight transformation.

TALONS

Since exploding in muscles, women swooned all over him, making her somewhat uncomfortable at times to be seen with him.

Kent stayed in the car while Gery went inside, took a window booth in Kent's direct line of sight and drank several cups of coffee to get warm while she waited. Kent's senses had grown keener with muscle mass and she knew he would sense danger if it was close.

An hour and fifteen minutes later, when Gery was sipping her final cup of coffee, Meg walked through the door. Food was stuck in her shiny hair which was more chocolate colored today than mousy as was its usual. Meg plopped onto the seat opposite Gery at the booth. Immediately, Gery noticed the pale, ashen color of her skin, and the gray swirling with the usual sapphire in her eyes. She appeared more beautiful in an I-will-eat-you-alive kind of way than Gery had ever noticed. The two of them had been nerd one and nerd two in college. Meg suddenly looked like a

TALONS

rock star and Gery still looked like Gery.

Without saying a word, Meg slid the vial across the table. "So, cloak and dagger. Now you really have me worried," voiced Gery.

Meg slid a bandana over her mouth and spoke in a low tone. "This sample could be truly dangerous. I believe the toxin in the blood can only be passed through the blood. I was exposed to it at work yesterday and I haven't felt right since. Please, be careful and let me know what you find."

Before Gery could speak another word, Meg was out the door and starting up her Jeep. She had moved so quickly Gery couldn't believe her eyes and sat still as a concrete statue while her mind tried to process what had just transpired between her and Meg. She had never seen her friend look so strangely attractive nor act so private. As fellow nerds, they had been each other's best friend since freshman year and now she felt Meg was holding back; hiding a horrible secret.

TALONS

Gery stowed the vial carefully inside her purse and walked back to her car. Kent had disappeared. Since sprouting huge muscles, his behavior had become more protective and even stalker-like at times. She knew he was staking out the area for harmful individuals. Patiently, she waited, as he turned up a few minutes later. He narrowed his eyes and looked directly into hers. A look she knew meant possible peril in the works. "Something followed her, an animal of some sort. Its musky odor is stinking up the air. Maybe we should follow her."

"Kent, that was the weirdest thing I've ever witnessed my friend do and this musky odor you smell. Maybe you need a shower," she said, trying to make light of the situation as she could feel tension hanging heavy enough in the air to cut it with a knife and dole out a portion to all of Alexandria, Virginia.

"Ha-ha, sis. You go home. I'm going to follow her."

"You're kidding? Without a car?"

TALONS

"I don't need one
and you wouldn't be
much help. Go analyze
whatever it was she
handed you." Then Kent
was running at max
speed.

Gery shook her head
in confusion and sped off
into the night. Kent had
his weird ways and so did
she. Gery was taking a
detour to her lab. The one
place in the world she felt
comfortable and safe.

Chapter 6

A strange set of green headlights had followed Meg to Alexandria. The vehicle had matched her pace exactly. It never got closer nor further away. Now two sets of headlights, one from behind and another, wingman, to her right, harmonized with the speed of her vehicle. She punched the accelerator in an effort to lose them, with no such luck. Finally, she resorted

TALONS

to pulling her vehicle over at a rest stop, turning off the headlamps and coasting into a parking space.

Her muscles were becoming tight and stiff. She had difficulty moving her joints, as if her body were going into a state of living rigor mortis. Meg willed her body to run. Instead, a mechanical jolting of her joints sent her skipping into the woods. The scent of iron and blood mingling with the crisp air filled her nostrils, dragging her rigid body along until it refused to work anymore.

Unwillingly, she fell beside a tree. Her body had given up, but her brain replayed the past twenty-four hours. The flying beast that had kidnapped and drugged her with his huge talon, and Amy. Her button nose and dark ringlets of hair that bounced when she skipped and laughed.

The virus was taking effect. It had given her strength at first, but now her body failed her and the end was coming soon. She'd never see her little angel again. Inside she cried, but no tears fell onto her cheeks as every

TALONS

part of her was giving up against her will.

Two green headlights showed behind the bushes of the forest. She knew they belonged to a someone not a something. A vehicle couldn't push into the terrain and the trees were too closely set. Her body was in a helpless state. The green eyes moved closer, out of the brush and into clear view. Her heart should have been pounding wildly; instead a faint bump erupted from her chest every several seconds, slowing with each moment she sat there, incapable of moving *thump... babump... thump*. Her death was finally happening and the green-eyed beast had come to finish the job the taloned beast hadn't.

The green-eyed beast moved closer and she could see a bush of fur hanging from its mouth. It dropped the bush of fur into her lap. She could feel its little heart beat every bit as faint and weak as her own, but couldn't move her head or arms to look at and touch it. The beast brought his nose to her face, sniffing her mouth,

TALONS

neck, and nuzzling its nose under her right armpit. Not with affection, more like double-checking something. At this close distance she could smell its breath, which carried the scent of flesh and iron; blood. She recognized the flavorful odor of blood. The creature was some type of large dog; possibly a wolf, but most likely a coyote. They were known to roam these woods. If her heart had been working it would have been beating a million miles a minute in fear. Instead it

continued its weary battle
*thump… babump…
thump…*
The beast took a few
steps backwards. Its body
began contorting and
twisting. Bones crunched
in such a way that she
could only imagine it
caused the beast
horrendous agony. Its
snout shrunk to the size
of a human nose, and hair
that had covered the
animal from head to toe
drew back inside its
pores. The claws that had
extended from the tips of
its paws disappeared
inside human flesh. In
front of her stood a dark,

TALONS

robust man. Had she
been able to scream, she
would have. Fear seized
whatever was left of her
heart.

The man knelt beside
her lifeless form. He took
the bush of fur, which
was a rabbit that he had
brought her, and raised it
above her head. He held
her mouth open and slit
the bunny from its neck
to its abdomen. The
blood rushed into her
mouth and spilled over,
trailing down her chin
and neck. He held his ear
to her chest and felt a
slight thump, enough to
know she was still alive.

Another wolf, most commonly mistaken in West Virginia area as a coyote, stepped out of the brush. The dark man picked her limp form off the ground and laid it on top of the other wolf. "Go, now. She doesn't have much time." The wolf nodded his understanding and raced off, bounding through the woods. The dark man morphed back into a wolf and took off after him.

TALONS

Chapter 7

eg awoke in what seemed to be a dungeon, as no windows were present. Within seconds her eyes adjusted to the darkness and she saw two figures; one the dark man from the woods, the other, in contrast, was light. Both were thick and muscular. She attempted to lift her arm and found she could. The rigor part of her illness had passed, or she was dead and dreaming.

Grabbing the soft blanket that was spread out over her she raised it to her chin, folding her body in terror and bringing her knees to her chest. The dark man spoke first.

"We found you in the woods. For now you are okay, but soon, very soon you will need to eat." He extended his hand. "I'm Semu." His actions were non-threatening. His voice told her he was sincere, but the past day and being locked in a dungeon with two bulky men made her continue with caution.

TALONS

Next, the light man spoke. "I'm Kent. We have been sent as your protectors. We can feel your fear but will not hurt you." He meant every word. He and Semu had been called to keep her safe. Had she stayed at home instead of running off in her harried state, they would have gathered her up and brought her here. Instead, they arrived at her home too late and had to sniff her out. Semu had discovered her first and trailed her to the coffee house.

Meg stared at them, dazed and lost. She had

no idea what they were talking about. In twenty-four hours, her life had gone from structured and predictable to insane crazy! Semu sat down beside her. "Stay away! I watched you change from an animal, a coyote, into a man. How?" she demanded.

Semu's lips turned up in a smile. "Yes, I did. We are not coyotes. We are wolves. More specifically, werewolves. We can change form. What you saw is correct." He had never been one to mix words and found, as a protector, it was best to be upfront and honest in order to gain trust.

He spoke with a gentle, intelligent voice, suddenly calming her nerves. Now questions remained. "How is that? What am I?"

Semu's smile disappeared while his dark mahogany eyes grew serious and directly met hers. "You have been chosen. Everyone here has been chosen for one purpose or another. Mine," he pointed to Kent, "ours, is to protect you."

She understood the gravity of his words but

couldn't grasp the why. "From what? My life was fine until a day ago when I was kidnapped by another creature I can't explain and drugged. You didn't answer my question -- what am I?" Her voice quivered with anger as all the danger and pain of the last twenty-four hours, along with the thought of never seeing Amy again, rose up inside her.

"You are a vampire in transformation. I fed you the blood of a rabbit. In order to survive, you need human blood. That human will be yours always."

Meg shook her head and starting hitting her cheeks. "I'm dreaming, this isn't real. My daughter is real. My job is real!"

Kent spoke up again. Her nerves were heightened again and she couldn't afford that. Not until the food arrived. In her weakened state, she wouldn't make it. He used his most soothing voice. "Antone, the creature who kidnapped you, is also a vampire. When you have finished your transformation you too will be able to fly. It takes a few lessons." A sly smile crept across his baby face. "His job is to turn other vampires. You are safe, and so is your daughter. No harm will come to her."

Meg babbled, "Gery, Gery, vial, oh my, shit." Running through her mind what would happen when Gery discovered the abnormalities in her blood -- that is if she was truly changing into a vampire and Kent had told the truth.

Kent pulled a small vial out of his pants pocket and placed it in the palm of his huge hand. ""You're worried about this?"

Meg took the vial and rolled it between her thumb and pointer finger. She was baffled by how the wolf had gotten hold of it. Her thoughts now turned to Gery and her safety. *Had these wolves harmed her in order to obtain it?* She would feel forever guilty if she had put her friend's life at risk. "How did you get this? Did you harm my friend?"

"No. Gery is my sister. I was there waiting in the car. When she came out I swapped the vials. The one she has is filled with ordinary human blood. She won't find anything." Kent knew Gery was trustworthy and the contents of the vial would have remained safe with her. It was the danger that Meg's blood would put Gery and all supernaturals in. He couldn't take the chance that someone else would get their hands on it. Supernaturals were mostly peaceful. It was the humans who were savage and both feared and desired the unknown.

Meg took in a deep breath and exhaled a sigh

TALONS

of relief. However, she was suddenly curious why werewolves and vampires were working together. *Weren't they sworn enemies?* "According to popular legends, werewolves and vampires have an intense dislike for one another. Why are you helping me?"

Semu's lips creased into another smile. "It is our job. Vampires and werewolves aren't enemies. Within each area, we work together. Like humans, we have factions on each continent. We don't always get along, wars break out." His smile left, lines burrowed across his forehead and his eyes narrowed. "Occasionally there are human casualties."

Kent spoke up, not allowing Meg the chance to reply. "Most of the legends you are familiar with are false, except one; werewolf blood will kill a vampire in minutes unless it's injected straight into the heart." He pointed his finger towards his chest. "That's why we can't feed you." Both Semu and Kent were hoping she would pick up on their subtle clues.

TALONS

Nobody spoke for a few minutes as they waited for Meg to fit the pieces together. A knock on the dungeon door interrupted the silence. A tall, slender, pale man opened the door and extended his hand to Meg. "I'm Frederic." She placed her hand in his then he lifted it to his lips and placed a soft kiss upon it. "You have become acquainted with Semu and Kent. Two of the finest protectors in our midst. Please, our hunters are back and we have a fine dinner for you

tonight and others for
you to meet."

TALONS

Chapter 8

Mesmerized by his voice, Meg trailed behind Frederic up a spiral staircase and into a beautiful foyer with marble floors and a giant, glittering chandelier. All the windows were tinted. She couldn't tell if it was day or night.

"Darling, make yourself comfortable." Frederic pointed to a hunter green velvet couch. Following his lead, she sat. Five women were brought out and lined up along the wall opposite her. Meg's mouth salivated and the only thing between her and their blood was Semu and Kent holding her back. They had her arms held tightly in their grasp.

Frederic looked into Meg's swirling sapphire, baby blue eyes and shook his head. "Darling, you have waited too long. This decision needs to have meaning. These women aren't only dinner but the one you choose will be yours for life. Her blood will sustain you and, in return, it will be physically impossible for you to drain her. Do you understand?" Meg nodded her head in agreement but all she smelled was dinner.

"Bring girl one forward," ordered Frederic as he took a seat on a green velvet chair that was a perfect match to the couch. He crossed his legs and leaned back into the velvety chair.

Another thin vampire brought forth the girl to Meg's far right. She was blonde and smelled like shit. Meg shook her head in disgust. Meg was beginning to understand.

She couldn't smell the
blood of the vampires
and the werewolves
carried a musky,
uninviting scent. A few
hours ago, all blood
smelled the same to her,
iron-y goodness that
drove her senses wild.
Now, all the odors from
these girls' blood swirled
in the air, one of them
smelled like cotton candy.
She was the one Meg
wanted, craved, and
would have. It was just as
Frederic said, she would
be sustained by one
human. A quirk of
evolution maybe, that
kept vampires from

TALONS

sucking the life out of
humans. One by one the
girls were brought to
Meg, she shook her head
at the first three. When
four was brought to her,
the sweet scent of her
blood curled through her
nostrils and on instinct
she lifted the girl's skirt
and sunk her pointy
newborn canines into her
flesh and sucked her
blood directly from her
femoral artery.

The warm blood
trickled down Meg's
throat with a steady flow.
She could feel her
muscles strengthen with
each drop of the girl's

sweet blood. Her heart went back to a regular rhythm *thump, thump, thump*. She regained her vitality and euphoria washed over her body like a drug. She had waited too long. From deep inside, a moan to wake the dead liberated itself from her lips. The meat she gorged on in the Jeep was a teaser. The pleasure she had felt miniscule compared to the magnitude she felt now. Her body convulsed with pure excitement as she let go of the girl's leg. Her nourishment complete, and desires peaking.

TALONS
Chapter 9

Meg writhed on the floor in ecstasy for several minutes. The vampires remembered their blood bonding and waited her out. The werewolves didn't understand but knew, as they had witnessed many vampires high after their first feeding. The young girl, Mayla, sat placidly on the velvet sofa. Her bright green almond eyes staring at a flaw in the wall. She too was feeling the bonding effects. Hours ago, Mayla had lived in a cardboard box on the street, shivering and cold she was thinking about how to get her next meal and wishing she was somewhere warmer as she wrapped her arms across the layered threadbare clothing around her chest.

A man more beautiful than any she had ever seen approached her. His dark hair curled in waves of thickness on top of his head. His light blue eyes oddly swirled with emerald green instead of flecks. She hadn't been able to take her eyes off

him. She felt drawn to
him. When he took her
hand and asked if she
would come with him to a
place with plenty of food,
her own private quarters,
and warmth, she didn't
resist. He was a complete
stranger and deep inside
she felt the danger of
going with him but she
didn't care. Nothing
could be worse than her
present predicament and
she felt a connection to
him. She knew she had to
go, something greater
than she had ever known
was about to happen.

He hadn't lied; when
they arrived at the place,

it was like a resort. She was first brought to a huge table with several others and a buffet of food; meats, vegetables, and fruit. She had always loved fruit because of its sweetness. It was like candy provided by nature. She stuffed her face until her belly was full; a feeling she hadn't felt in weeks.

She and the others were then brought down a hallway containing a series of rooms, each was given a room number and told that was their permanent home. The twin bed was soft and

TALONS

inviting. The closet was stuffed with name brand clothes and shoes just her size and the bathroom was stocked with shampoo, conditioner, toothpaste, lotions, toilet paper, soft towels, and her own toothbrush and hairbrush. The window in her room looked out onto a mammoth-sized indoor pool that looked like something a rich and famous Hollywood star might have in their home. She couldn't believe her luck!

The high wore off and Meg pulled herself up and sat next to the girl.

She had no idea what to say to her. The girl took her eyes off the flaw in the wall and stared deeply into Meg's. For several seconds, the two stared into each other's eyes. Their souls were bonding and each's memories were filling the other's head. It was a telepathic transmission and part of the bonding process. Meg took Mayla's hand and mentally spoke into her head, *I'm Meg. I see and feel all your thoughts and memories. I know you've been hurt, but now you are forever safe. So long as I live, so will you.*

TALONS

Mayla responded, *I know. I felt it when the beautiful dark haired man spoke to me and invited me here. I connected with him and felt his compassion. I'm Mayla.*

Meg had seen the dark haired man in her head. The vision had brought her peace inside for the first time after the past few years of pain. He was alive. Before she could finish her thought, Frederic interrupted. "Ladies, you will have more time later to continue your private discussion. Mayla, please return to your quarters.

Meg, I need you to come with me. There is someone who has waited to see you. His wait has been long enough." He held a door framed in gold molding open and waited for her to pass through.

The room Meg entered was huge and many other vampires were seated and mingling. Crown molding framed the vaulted ceiling and the decor was modern but elegant. There were no windows. The only light was artificial illumination from the black and silver five-head floor lamps

TALONS

posted in the eight corners of the octagon shaped room. Frederic took her hand, it was as cold as hers, and led her to a loveseat where he asked her to wait. She seated herself on the loveseat while her heart beat wildly with expectation and longing.

Chapter 10

Arms she remembered well and craved wrapped around her neck from behind. Soft lips placed gentle kisses upon her cheek and neck forcing her toes to curl with excitement. His lips brushed her ear and he whispered, "I missed you, come with me and let me show you how much." Her body shuddered in response. Meg took his hand and followed him to a private room. She wanted to know how he was still alive and why he hadn't contacted her or visited Amy. Those questions and answers would come later. Now she wanted and needed him.

The room she followed him to was devoid of windows and contained modern furnishings with a queen-sized bed covered in silk sheets that begged her to lay down and allow her husband, Mr. Vince Mercer, to have his way. He lay down beside her and caressed her glowing, pale skin as he tenderly pulled her shirt off and caressed her pale flesh that had been hidden underneath. He then proceeded to roll her pants down while she met his actions and stripped him of his clothes.

Their tongues swirled and played against each other's skin and lips. Vince traced his tongue around her nipples then down her abdomen and teased her clit. She ran her fingers through his hair as she fought such an early climax. He lifted his torso and brought his cock against her entrance, then plunged inside her.

TALONS

Within a moment her body shuddered in a bliss that matched his. Their vampiric abilities and longing for one another allowed them to carry on, climaxing several times. Each relished what they hadn't had in over four years, yet yearned for more.

Hours later, the glow from the lamp made a small circle of light on the wall. Silken sheets sagged off the bed while Meg and Vince held each other closely after they had filled each other with love. Meg's head rested on Vince's chest, counting each beat of his heart. "What happened babe?" she asked in a voice, little above a whisper.

He smoothed her bangs across her forehead. "I was in danger. The man that killed all those people was a vampire gone rogue. The bars of the jail cell wouldn't hold him for long and his being there endangered all supernaturals. I was kidnapped, vampire blood injected under my arm, and brought here. During my transformation, everything was explained to me."

"Vampire blood is what they inject us with?"

Vince chuckled. "Yes. That is the only way to turn a human. Did you think we suck their blood and suddenly they became a vampire?"

She gently slapped his chest. "No. I knew I was injected with something, I just didn't know what."

"Ouch," he responded to her playful slap. "Humans need vampire blood to turn, and to finish the transition a new born vamp has to eat. Did you enjoy Mayla?"

"I did," she responded with joy. "She was tasty. How did you know?"

The corners of his sensuous lips turned up into a smile. "I chose her and the others. We choose a human for each palate of the tongue; sweet, salty, bitter, sour, and MSG. Sometimes our taste buds change after we turn, but yours didn't. You have always had a sweet tooth, so when I smelled Mayla I knew instantly she would be your choice."

TALONS

She twisted the clump of curly hairs on Vince's chest as she asked, "Please, go on with your story?"

"The shape shifters can take the form of any organism, so they snuck into his cell and injected his heart with werewolf venom. He died instantly. My regret was missing you and Amy. My solace was knowing you were safe. The rogue vampire was dead. Our faction is in need of another doctor -- that is how I got you here. We all have jobs. I gather humans. My training in psychology and heightened vampiric senses make me perfect for collecting humans. They naturally trust me." His voice trailed off as he wished Amy could join them.

Meg was thinking identical thoughts. She wanted her daughter. "Is there a job for Amy?"

"She is too young. We age slowly." The sad tone of his voice gave away his thoughts. Meg knew him too well.

"Can we bring her here to live with the other humans?" Without giving him a chance to respond, she continued, "The humans do stay here, right?"

"Yes, this is their home. They want for nothing and any small desires they have are fulfilled. They have a small community on the other side of the property."

An idea formulated in her head. She saw Elsa and Amy living in the human community until Amy was old enough to become a vampire. "Who do we talk to? Amy needs to be here with us."

"Frederic."

Chapter 11

"I had already anticipated your request. A child needs their parents. Sit, relax. I have a story," Frederic suggested as he turned his black, padded swivel chair in the direction of Meg and Vince. His sharp vampiric senses had alerted him of their presence.

The Mercer's sat opposite Frederic in matching thickly padded, burgundy leather chairs. Frederic leaned forward

TALONS

and folded his hands
together upon his large,
solid mahogany desk. His
eyes flashed from Meg to
Vince and back to Meg.
"It was my father who
founded this place. He
was turned and used his
great wealth to build all
this. I was merely a child
when this happened. My
mother was killed the
night my father was
turned. It was during
times of human war."

The blue, telltale
vampire swirl in his eye lit
up as he continued to
reminisce. "My father
begged for my older sister
and I to be brought to

him. It wasn't customary even then, but the huge heart of our vampire leader, Jackson, relented. He allowed it. We soon came here to America and he set all this up. It has been modernized through the years. We lived with him and grew up in a vampire world. When we turned seventeen, we were given the choice of being turned. I chose to become a vampire and inherit all this. My sister had fallen in love with Henry, a vampire, and chose to be his. Today they live in the southern faction." Frederic leaned

TALONS

back in his chair and swiveled to face a painting of the countryside – the only trace of the outside world that was available, since few windows dotted the walls of the mansion.

Frederic stood up. Meg and Vince's eyes followed his movements. "Amy and her nanny, Elsa, will be brought here. I have sent a collector and given them strict orders to bring them to me. We will discuss the necessary arrangements and set them up in the human community. You need to understand that Elsa has a choice. We don't believe in forcing people."

Meg's eyes, anxious upon their meeting with Frederic, now softened with gratitude. "Thank-you, this means so much to us."

Vince stood and grabbed Frederic's hand, then slipped his arm around his back in a quick man-hug. "This means everything to my wife and I."

TALONS

Epilogue

Thirteen years later...

Amy left her quarters, giving Elsa a hug then proceeded to the large house. Her thick chocolate curls bounced as she walked into the grand room decorated with thickly padded green velvet furniture. She had known the risks of her decision and had even seen a few vampires go through transition. Her parents felt it was an important experience to assist her in making the decision to become a vampire or not. Frederic had a taken a special liking to her. He had become something of a surrogate grandfather, so when she requested only one human be brought to her, he obliged.

She had chosen Jimmy. He had been brought to the compound only a couple of years after her, under similar circumstances. They had quickly become best friends and had many times discussed this moment. She always knew she would choose to be a vampire and he would

TALONS

forever be her human. As he walked into the room, his blood smelled delicious. As she brought her mouth to his flesh, she was surprised at how sharp canines sprouted from her gums and sank into the flesh surrounding his femoral artery. His blood ran rich and creamy down her throat and awoke her near dead body.

Talons is one story from Winter Thrillz 1, only available in ebook. Keep reading for the first two chapters of Tigress.

TALONS

Tigress

Chapter 1

Jestin turned his truck onto the gravel road, the snow around him dusting the earth beneath the tires. The snowy retreat just what he needed after defending the asshole he knew had killed his wife in cold blood. It was his job. Times like these, he wished he stood on the other side, defending the victim, but many times the defendant was the

victim. DNA now proved
so many people were
wrongly convicted, and
then there were the ones
like Trevor Bolling.

The evidence was all
circumstantial, nothing
tied him to the murder
and he conjured real tears
when his wife's name
came up. He did his job
and Trevor's case was
dropped. It was his
demeanor, the smirk on
his face, the twisting of
his hands, and his
arrogant attitude. If he'd
put him on the stand, his
attitude alone would have
convicted him. But his

job was to defend his client, guilty or innocent.

The snow falling faster now, making Jestin creep his vehicle over the snowy gravel toward the cabin at a snail's pace. A light dusting now covered the trees. His phone beeped, causing him to look away from the road for a second. His eyes scanned the message, work related. He dropped the phone onto the passenger seat, not willing to work when he was on vacation. The purpose of the trip was to get away from work and stress.

TALONS

When he lifted his eyes to the road, a white flash in front of him caught his attention. "What the..." His voice trailed off as he stopped the car and got out, thinking maybe he'd hit something. A fresh set of paw prints crossed the road from one side of the woods to the other. Not much of a hunter, he wasn't sure what type of animal. From his trips to the zoo as a child, they looked to him like tiger prints -- but tigers didn't exist in Virginia except in the zoo. Scratching his head, he got back into the car and continued up the snow-laden road.

He thought of all the animals that lived in these woods; black bears, foxes, raccoons, deer, and skunks. It wasn't any of those. A wolf maybe. *Did they inhabit the woods here?*

A majestic white animal stared at him as he studied the ground then resumed his drive. Its violet eyes narrowed.

TALONS

Chapter 2

Jestin pulled into the horseshoe drive of the cabin and stepped out of the vehicle, sucking in the clean, chilly air surrounding him. His eyes scanning the area for animals, namely the one he was sure he'd seen but nothing except quiet and snow covered trees.

He stretched and opened the back door of his oversized truck, reached in and pulled out

his luggage, carrying it up
the small covered porch
to the front door. He
dropped it and fiddled
with his key in the lock. A
crackling sound from the
woods forced him to
twist his head in that
direction. He saw
nothing. The sound was
barely audible, it was
nothing.

Inside, he dropped
his bag. Leaving the door
open, he made a couple
trips to and from his car,
his arms filled with
groceries. The air outside
growing dark, he went to
the shed before the sun
set completely for the day

TALONS

and grabbed an armful of
firewood. The cabin
inside was cold and he
needed to get the fire
roaring before the
temperature dropped
further. The snow now
inches thick, he trudged
to the cabin and laid the
load of wood near the
fireplace, then considered
if he should get more.
The snow outside now
coming down much
heavier than earlier.

Even inside his thick
coat, he shivered and
decided against bringing
in more wood now; he'd
do it in the morning.
Locking the door and

dropping the bar across it, he went straight to building a fire. Warmth first, food second.

Three hours later, he finished dinner, took a bite off a piece of cornbread that went with the chili he'd made and stared blankly into the snow. The white flash of the animal he'd seen earlier high on his thought list. There wasn't one white animal he could think of that lived in the woods, unless it was a wolf. It had to be a wolf, which meant there were more. Wolves weren't singular animals but plural, they moved in packs.

A shotgun leaned against the log wall beside the door. He had protection if it was a wolf. He didn't hunt, but could fire a bullet straight into the heart or head of anything. His dad had taught him since he was a boy, hoping to make him a hunter. Jestin didn't have the heart. He was a softie who loved life. Again, the case with Trevor Bolling haunted him.

Drawing open the curtain in his room so the sun would shine bright in the morning and wake him early, he lay in bed, fighting his thoughts about work, and went to sleep.

His sleep burdened with his own guilt, he tossed and turned, finally waking. The light of the crescent moon filtering through the window, casting a glow. Fluffing the pillow beneath his head, he turned toward the open window, two violet eyes stared back at him.

TALONS